TiME TWiSTER

This is a work of fiction and any resemblance of characters to persons living or dead is purely coincidental.

Many of the designations used by manufacturers and sellers to distinguish their products are claimed as trademarks. Where those designations appear in this book and Kids Can Press Ltd. was aware of a trademark claim, the designations have been printed in initial capital letters (e.g., Godzilla).

Kids Can Press acknowledges the financial support of the Government of Ontario, through the Ontario Media Development Corporation's Ontario Book Initiative.

Published in Canada by
Kids Can Press Ltd.
29 Birch Avenue
Toronto, ON M4V 1E2

Published in the U.S. by
Kids Can Press Ltd.
2250 Military Road
Tonawanda, NY 14150

www.kidscanpress.com

Edited by Tara Walker
Designed by Karen Powers
Printed and bound in Canada

CM 08 0 9 8 7 6 5 4 3 2 1
CM PA 08 0 9 8 7 6 5 4 3 2 1

Library and Archives Canada Cataloguing in Publication

Asch, Frank
Time twister : journal #3 of a cardboard genius / by Frank Asch.

ISBN 978-1-55453-230-8 (bound)
ISBN 978-1-55453-231-5 (pbk.)

I. Title.

PZ7.A778Ti 2008 j813'.54 C2007-904099-3

Kids Can Press is a Corus™ Entertainment company

TiME TWiSTER

JOURNAL #3 OF A CARDBOARD GENIUS

by Frank Asch

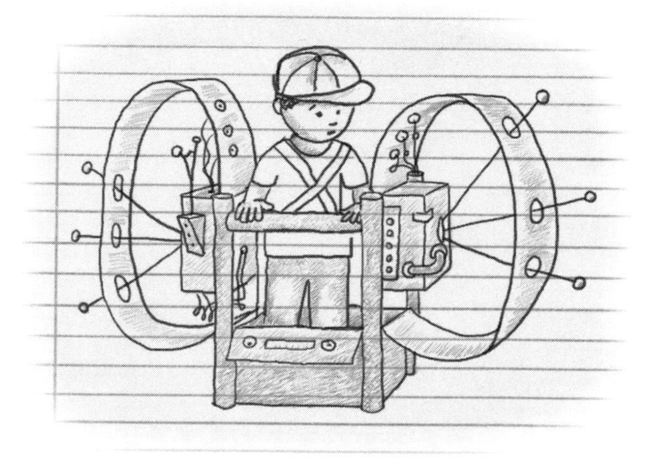

Kids Can Press

To Nicholas, Andre, Levi and Caleb Yoder

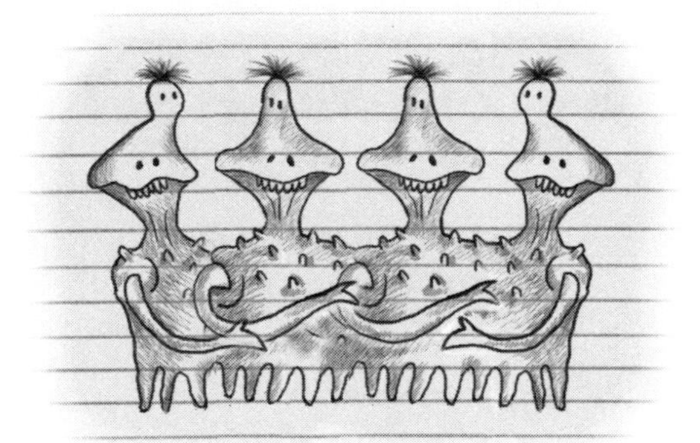

Table of Contents

CHAPTER 1

A Hitch in Time

First — five important facts:

Fact #1: This is my third incredible journal. I write in it whenever I can steal a few minutes from my hyper-busy life to share my genius with the rest of the humdrum world. Consider yourself lucky to be reading it!

Fact #2: I'm probably the smartest human being on Earth. If you doubt that, just ask yourself what other scientist in the world today has single-handedly achieved the stupendous feat of constructing the world's first intergalactic spaceship mostly out of ordinary cardboard boxes!

Fact #3: I'm about to leave Planet Earth and explore the universe in my spaceship, Star Jumper, with the girl who sits in front of me in study hall. Her name is Zoe, and she's really neat.

Fact #4: My little brother, Jonathan, is a rat-demon, psychopathic creep-slug of pure evil!

Fact #5: I finally tamed that rotten little snake. Not completely, of course. (Some things, after all, *are* impossible!) But enough to make Jonathan tolerable. And it was *so* easy. All I had to do was tell him he could come with me when I leave Planet Earth.

Ever since I came up with that lovely little lie, Jonathan has been falling over backward to keep on my good side. Every morning he pours my orange juice for me. He feeds my goldfish without being asked. He's quiet when he walks past my door. He stops asking questions when I tell him to shut up. He doesn't try to get me in trouble with Mom and Dad. And he doesn't insist on sitting next to me on the school bus anymore. He's even stopped calling me names like "poopy face" and shoving hate mail under my door!

That's the good news. The bad news is that we've hit yet another snag in our mission. Yep, it's happened again! Just when I thought Star Jumper was ready for final blast-off, a totally new and unexpected problem popped up.

This time Zoe discovered the hitch. After she finished maneuvering Star Jumper around my bedroom in Lift-Off Mode, Zoe expertly landed her on my bedroom rug, climbed out the main portal and sat beside me while I did some equipment checks.

"Nice work, Zoe," I said. "Now you'll be able to take over in an emergency."

"I'm still a little shaky with the gyro-stick," she announced with a sigh.

"Don't worry, you'll get the hang of it," I reassured her.

We were quiet for a while, and then Zoe cleared her throat and said, "Um … Last night I read a little article on the Internet about relativity."

Zoe is mainly interested in biology and zoology, but she's curious about all sorts of things.

"That's great," I said. "The more astrophysics you know, the better."

"Well … I can't exactly say I understood it all. In fact, most of it went right over my head. But one detail kind of stuck out."

I was double-checking some batteries to make sure they were fresh. As incredible as it may sound, Star Jumper's Stellar Drive works on just two AA batteries. But they have to be operating at full capacity for the quantum leap effect to function properly.

"It said Einstein predicted interstellar space travel will warp one's sense of time," Zoe continued in a casual tone of voice. "Do you know anything about that?"

Einstein is my hero. I know everything there is to know about him and his theories.

"Sure, I know all about that stuff," I said.

I took the batteries from the special recharger I had constructed from old radio parts and slid them into place. Then I turned on Star Jumper's operating system. Full capacity! I picked up my clipboard and crossed off "check batteries."

"So is it true that time seems to pass differently for anyone traveling at the speed of light?" she asked.

"It doesn't just *seem* to pass differently," I replied. "It *does* pass differently."

I did my best to explain without math. "You see, time and space are connected so they interact relative to one another." I even gave her an example. "Take two watches showing the same time. Put one of them in a spaceship and shoot it across the galaxy and back again at the speed of light. When that watch returns it will show a different time than the watch that stayed behind on Earth."

Zoe blew a strand of long, dark brown hair out of her face. "That's *exactly* what it said on the Internet."

"So why are you asking me questions if you already know the answers?" I asked. *Is Zoe playing games with me?* I wondered.

Space/Time Warp

"I just wanted to know if *you* knew," she replied.

"Of course I know! Einstein had it all figured out in 1915 in his general theory of relativity."

I was getting a little annoyed.

"So how much time will have passed for people on Earth when we return from our interstellar trip?" asked Zoe. "Do you know *that*?"

"Well ... no. I never bothered to crunch the numbers. But I'm sure it's not much," I said, wondering what Zoe was getting at.

"Never *bothered*?"

"Well, I just assumed it would be minutes, hours, maybe even a few days."

"Oh!" she said, raising her voice a notch or two. "You *assumed*, did you? That's not very *scientific*, is it?"

"Well —" I began, but Zoe didn't give me a chance to explain. I had never seen her so worked up.

"Could it be a week?" she pressed.

"Theoretically, yes," I replied. "It could be. But —"

"How about a month — or a year? How about ten years? Twenty years? How about a *hundred* years?"

At last I could see where Zoe was going with all this.

I was about to say, “That’s ridiculous. It couldn’t possibly be that long.” But then I stopped myself. I had to admit that I didn’t really know how time would pass on Earth while we were away.

I reached for the little notebook and pencil I always have on hand and made some quick calculations.

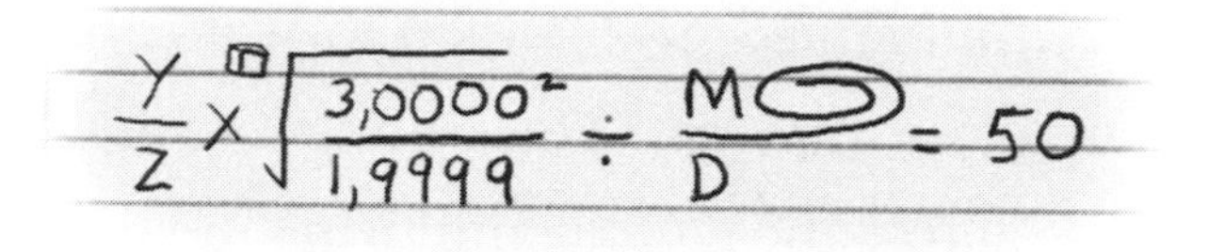

The Formula

“Hmmm … This is interesting. According to these calculations,” I said, trying not to sound too concerned, “even if we find a suitable planet on our first or second try and return in what will be only six or seven days for us, everyone we left behind on Earth will be … er … um … approximately fifty years older.”

CHAPTER 2

Time Out

"Fifty years!" Zoe squealed as if I had just thrown scalding hot water on her. "That's a *long* time!"

"Yeah, well, not in geological terms. After all, Earth is more than four billion years old —"

"Never mind that!" She leaned forward and put her face up close to mine. "You were going to take me halfway across the galaxy and bring me back fifty years from now!"

"I told you, I never did the calculations," I said in my own defense.

"That's no excuse!" Zoe's face turned bright red and her freckles got darker looking. "If you think I'm willing to go away with you and come back to a world where all my friends are over sixty years old, you're crazy!" Then she added pleadingly, "Alex, why didn't you tell me?"

"I just *did* tell you!"

"You didn't tell me!" she snarled. "I had to ask! That's not the same, and you know it!"

Suddenly I was angry, too. How ungrateful could someone be? Here I was, the greatest genius the world has ever known, offering Zoe the chance to participate in the most stupendous scientific experiment of all time! And she was turning me down because of what it might do to her *social* life?

"Fine!" I shouted. "If you don't want to come with me, don't. I'll go alone. Live your life like everyone else. Be an earthworm! I don't care. I'm going to see new places and do new things no one on Earth has ever dreamed of before!"

Zoe glared at me incredulously. "Even though when you come back everyone you know now could be dead?"

"So what?" I said. "There will be new people to share my discoveries with!"

"And you can go down in history as the greatest scientist that ever lived!" she shouted.

"That's right," I said. "Because that's precisely what I am!"

"Then you certainly don't need little old me around, do you?!" she hollered. "And another thing," she said, lowering her voice to a mere whisper. "I think the way you treat your little brother is despicable!"

The next thing I knew Zoe had stomped out of my room, slamming the door behind her.

That last bit about Jonathan really did it! How *dare* she criticize how I treat that little monster!

I flopped down on my bed and stewed. *So Zoe's not coming with me. Okay. No problem,* I told myself. *Heck! I don't need her. I'll go by myself. That's all. It's simple. Who needs a boring Earth girl as a companion anyway? I'll be visiting lots of planets before I pick the one where I want to live. Along the way I'll meet plenty of interesting aliens who will jump at the chance to travel with me. Perhaps I'll find a two-headed traveling companion who knows lots of extraterrestrial languages and*

Two-Headed Translator

customs: one head will listen to me and translate while the other head will advise me about what to say and how to act.

Or maybe I'll hook up with a superior plant being who can grow me tasty snacks whenever I get hungry.

Or maybe I'll befriend an armored crablike creature who will become my faithful sidekick and defend me whenever I'm in danger.

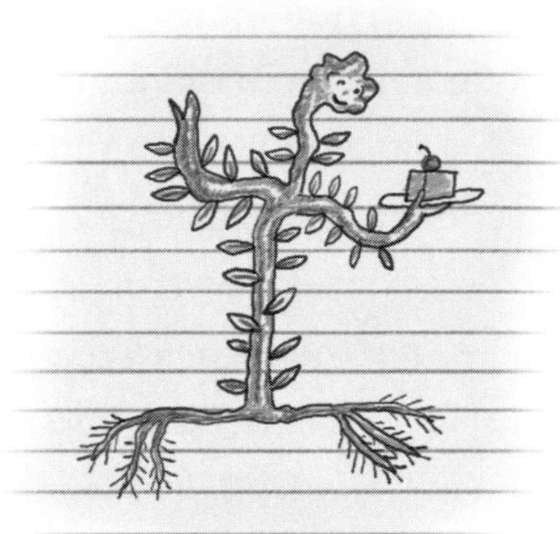

Snack Being

Bodyguard

I was totally immersed in my thoughts about how great it was going to be on my new planet when Jonathan sauntered into the room.

"How may I serve you, sir?" he asked with a sickly sweet smile.

Lately, Jonathan's been overdoing his nice brother act, calling me names like "sir" and "honorable one." At the dinner table the other night he jumped up and pushed in my chair as if I were an old lady! That night when I went to bed I found a tiny foil-wrapped chocolate on my pillow!

"Drop dead," I answered.

"Yes, sir," he replied and collapsed onto the floor in a heap.

"Very funny," I said. "Now get out of here."

The contorted pile of arms and legs moved, and one eye peeked out from under Jonathan's blue baseball cap. "Really?"

"REALLY!" I shouted. "Get out of here!"

"Okay! Okay! Don't have a heart attack! I'm

leaving, I'm leaving!" he protested and picked himself up off the floor. Then, bowing deeply, he walked backward out of my door and into the hall. "Please let your humble servant know if you need anything. Anything at all."

"I need you to shut the door!" I hollered. "Right now!"

Jonathan pressed his hands together and bowed even deeper.

"As you wish, intelligent one," he said and slowly shut my door.

I waited to hear the sound of his footsteps leaving but there was none. He just stood outside my door for a moment. Then he said in a low whisper, "I heard you and Zoe fighting."

Jonathan is always spying on me. Sometimes I think he knows more about me than I know about myself.

"Get lost, Jonathan!" I said.

"I just want to say it's okay that she's not coming with us," he replied.

Us, I thought. *That's a laugh! I'd sooner stuff my pants with scorpions and tarantulas than take him anywhere!*

"Don't worry. I can be your copilot," he added. "I know everything Zoe knows and more!"

"You aren't going anywhere with me if you don't get away from my door!" I shouted. "Right now!"

"Okay! Okay! I'm leaving," he said, and finally I heard footsteps going down the hall.

CHAPTER 3

Doing Time

I don't usually have trouble falling asleep, but that night I did. I knew I should be happy. My ultimate dream was about to come true. Soon I'd be traveling to another planet where I'd never have to see Jonathan's creepy little face again! I should have been *deliriously* happy. But my sheets felt stiff and scratchy. And my pillow, which up until then had never given me the slightest problem, suddenly developed a bad case of the lumps.

I kept thinking about what Zoe had said. The more I went over her words in my mind the more I realized she had a point. I didn't want to come back to a world fifty years older than the one I had left either.

So I hopped out of bed and cracked open my relativity notebook. I checked and double-checked my earlier calculations. The answers I got were exactly the same as before. If anything, the results were worse!

"We're prisoners! Prisoners of time!" I moaned.

Just then I happened to glance into the small mirror I keep on the bureau next to my desk. "Wait a minute!" I said to the smart young face in the mirror. "Who's the world's greatest supergenius?" I paused to admire my good looks, my intelligent brow and penetrating eyes. Then I grinned at myself. "YOU are! That's who!"

The World's Greatest Supergenius

But the world's greatest genius had just run into the world's greatest problem: changing the laws of Mother Nature.

If only I had a time machine, I thought. Then it hit me.

"That's it!" I cried. "A time machine! I don't have to change the laws of nature. I just have to build a time machine to get around them!"

It was so simple. I don't know why I didn't think of it earlier. A time machine moves matter backward and forward through time. So of course it could cancel out the time shift factor! With a time machine Zoe and I could leave Earth after breakfast, travel at the speed of light (186,000 miles per second) anywhere in the universe for months at a time and be back for lunch. It was a perfect solution!

I spent the rest of the night working on the theoretical problems of time travel. And what a night it was! I left my bedroom only three times:

once to pee, once to get more paper and once to sharpen my pencil. Hours passed like minutes. Talk about time distortion! The next thing I knew, morning light was streaming in my bedroom window.

My back ached. I had cramps in my fingers, and my butt was sore. But I also had a theory and, even better, a basic design for a time machine! And I was pretty sure it would work.

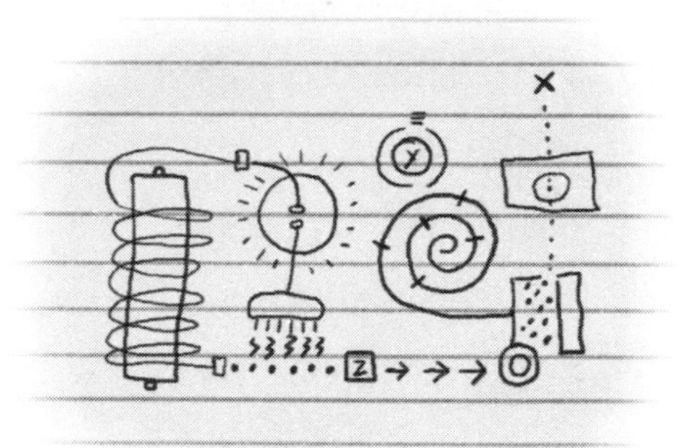

My Basic Design

I had just gotten dressed when Jonathan came to my door with his cap on crooked and his eyes all puffy.

"Last night Merlin and I collected poison toads in the full moon together," he announced.

I'm sure the creep thought he was being nice to me. But I found all his nonsense about his favorite storybook character, Merlin the magician, stupid and annoying. "Then a dragon came, and it got pretty scary."

"Yeah, sure," I said as I tossed my pajamas in the hamper. "Oh, and for your information, the moon wasn't full last night. It was in first quarter."

"That's strange," replied Jonathan, wrinkling his brow. "It was a full moon in Camelot."

"Is that so?" I said and bounded downstairs to the kitchen, determined not to let Jonathan destroy my good mood.

CHAPTER 4

Time and Time Again

Breakfast that morning was the usual torment, only in reverse. Allow me to explain. You see, Jonathan used to eat like a pig. Then overnight he went from slob to snob! Instead of shoving food in his mouth like a bulldozer filling in a deep hole, he now sups with the manners of a prince.

Take, for example, the way he used to eat pancakes. First he'd tilt back his head and drape a pancake over his face. Then, using only his tongue and teeth, he'd suck the pancake into his mouth. Now he slices his pancakes into tiny pieces on his plate with fine silverware. He coats the pieces one at a time in butter and syrup. Then he chews each bite thoroughly with his mouth closed. Finally, he swallows with a smile, takes a tiny sip of orange juice and dabs his lips gingerly with a satin napkin. (It has to be satin!)

The Old Way

Jonathan used to snarf food from the table, his chair and even the floor. But now he refuses to dine off anything but the finest china. And he insists that Mom light a candelabra for him at every meal, even breakfast!

The New Way

On the plus side, these newfound manners, disturbing as they are, don't turn my stomach to the point of retching. But what's really mind-boggling is how Mom and Dad put up with all this!

"Don't you think there's something weird about Jonathan's new eating habits?" I asked Mom as she plunked down a second stack of pancakes in front of me.

"Not really," she answered with a smile. "Jonathan is still exploring boundaries of social acceptability, that's all."

Boundaries of social acceptability? What could I say to that? Mom and Dad are both psychiatrists. So it's no wonder they don't have much common sense when it comes to raising a six year old.

"How about I take my breakfast up to my room?" I asked.

But Dad nixed that idea. "It would be nice if we all ate at the same table," he said. Togetherness breeds togetherness."

Togetherness breeds togetherness? What's that supposed to mean?

I rolled my eyes and complained, "I just don't like looking at him!"

"Try turning your chair away," suggested Mom.

So that's what I did. I ate my entire breakfast with my back to my brother, looking at the little blue and white flowers on our kitchen wallpaper.

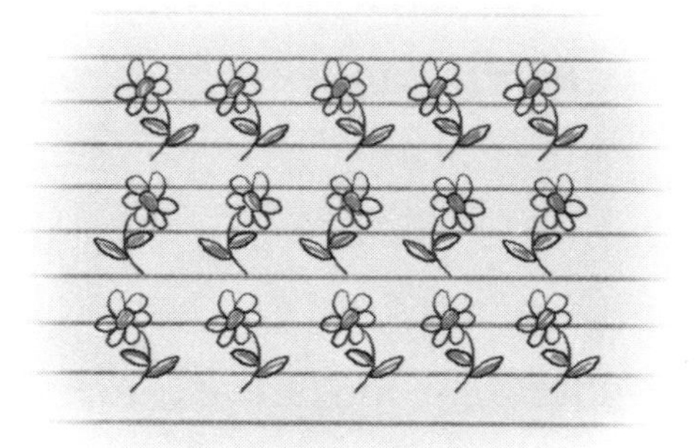

After breakfast I ran upstairs, eager to get to work on my time machine.

While I wired up a series of wine corks, paper clips, lead washers and rubber erasers to make a unified field sequencer, Jonathan wandered in.

Unified Field Sequencer

"My room's too cold. Can I stay in yours?"

"What are you talking about?" I said. "It's May, for crying out loud! Mom's got all the windows open."

"I know, but I'm cold," he said. "And besides, now that Zoe's not coming with us you're going to need my help getting ready."

I seriously doubted that. But I guess I was in a really good mood because I let him stay.

"Okay, you can stick around. But you have to behave," I warned him. "One false move, one annoying question or comment and you're out. And don't touch anything! Got it?"

Jonathan smiled.

"Got it!" he said and then quickly added, "Your wondrous one."

"And stop trying to be so nice. It's irritating!"

"Your wish is my command, Master," he replied with a low bow.

This new Jonathan was really getting on my nerves, but I have to admit he was pretty good at keeping his word. He sat quietly for over half an hour browsing through one of my scientific notebooks while I worked on the time machine. He turned and studied the pages slowly as if he understood them. *Let him read my calculations,* I thought. *There's no way he can really understand them.*

When I had installed the field sequencer I got out my aluminum foil collection — a giant ball of used foil almost two feet in diameter that I've been collecting for years. I unwrapped some of the foil and molded it into a half-inch-thick rod that I wrapped around the outside of the field sequencer.

I secured the foil with brass fasteners, and the time warp antenna was complete. After adding the power source — one D battery — my first time machine prototype was ready to test!

Finally, Jonathan spoke up. "So what are you making, Alex?"

It's my policy never to tell Jonathan more than I need to. "It's a new kind of eraser," I lied.

"Oh, yeah?" he replied. "Show me how it works."

"Okay," I said and drew an X with my pencil on a small scrap of notebook paper. Then I placed the paper in the time-warp chamber. "Watch that X."

My First Prototype

I activated the chrono-sensors and flipped on the field sequencer.

Jonathan leaned forward and stared at the X.

Slowly the pencil marks on the paper "undrew" themselves. It looked as if they were being erased. But they were actually being undone, like a film running backward.

It was just a small trip through time. Not much mass was involved. But my first test was a complete and utter success! My prototype wasn't a full-fledged time machine capable of sending a human being backward and forward through time. But my theory and principles were working.

And to think I had made all this progress in less than a day! Once again I astounded myself! Now all that remained was to construct the real thing.

CHAPTER 5

Time Twister

"So that's it?" said Jonathan. "You made a new kind of eraser?"

"Yep, that's it," I said. "Pretty neat, eh?"

"That's a lot of baloney!" said Jonathan, screwing his face up so he looked like a nasty pit bull. "You didn't erase that X. You sent it back in time."

"Huh?" I was so stunned I couldn't think of what to say.

"You think you're so smart and I'm so stupid!" he yelled. "But I know a time machine when I see one!"

Sometimes, I have to admit, it's downright creepy how smart the creep really is!

"Time machine. That's rich," I lied.

I half expected the little monster to kick me or something. That's what the old Jonathan would have done. Getting even — that's what he was all about. But the new Jonathan was different. "Don't worry," he said. "I won't tell. I never have and I never will. I just want to help."

The fact was, now that my prototype was a success, I needed a live subject to test out a full-scale model. I didn't own any mice, rabbits or monkeys. And I was not about to risk the life of my pet goldfish, Einstein.

"Okay," I sighed. "You can help."

Jonathan couldn't believe I was giving in so easily. He knitted his eyebrows and stuck out his lower lip.

"Really?" he asked suspiciously. "No tricks?"

"Really," I replied. "No tricks! But you have to actually help. Whatever I tell you to do you have to do it! No complaints or whining!"

"You got it, boss!" Jonathan took off his cap and threw it in the air. "No complaints or whining!" Then he jumped on my bed, knocking my pillow on the floor. (I hate it when he does that.)

The first order of business was to make a time-warp chamber large enough for a person. The cardboard boxes used to ship refrigerators would have been perfect. But I didn't have one. What I did have were several small boxes, some cardboard wrapping-paper rolls and lots of duct tape.

"Okay, first thing," I spat out my first command. "Fetch me all the cardboard boxes in the cellar!"

"Right away, oh generous one!" exclaimed Jonathan, and he flew out of the room.

With Jonathan's help running various errands and handing me tools, work on the second prototype went quicker than I expected. By three o'clock it was ready to test.

"All right," I said to Jonathan. "Here's how it's going to work. You get in the box, and I'll adjust the controls. If everything functions the way it's supposed to, you'll go backward in time. Let's see ..." — I adjusted the time markers — "about five minutes."

"Five minutes?" He scrunched up his face. "Is that *all*?"

"It's just a test," I said. "Your job is to pay attention and report back about the experience." I handed him a notebook and pencil. "Take notes."

"I can't spell," he said.

"Doesn't matter," I told him. "Draw pictures if you want. Ready?"

"Right now?"

"Yep, right now," I said. "Step right into my chrono-dymaxi-space/time-multiphaser."

"Boy, that's a real tongue twister," said Jonathan.

"Actually it's a *time* twister," I said and helped him into the machine.

"Hey, that's a good name," said Jonathan. "Can we call it Time Twister instead of — you know — whatever it was you just said … chrono-dymax … something or other?"

"Call it whatever you want," I said and buckled him in with a makeshift safety harness fashioned from two of Dad's old leather belts.

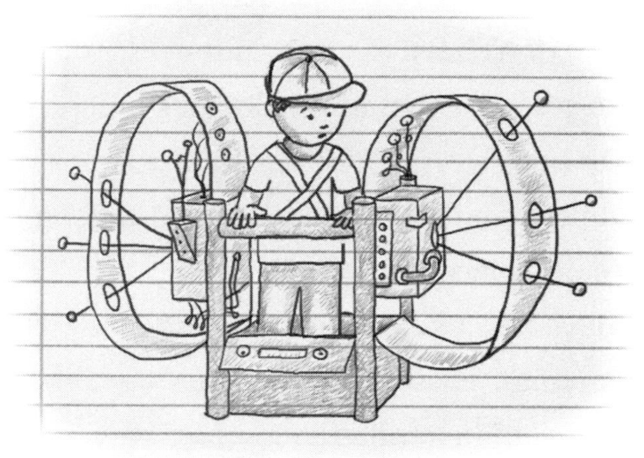

Time Twister

"This Time Twister isn't dangerous, is it?" he asked as I tightened the harness. "I mean … How come I'm the one testing it first?"

"Believe me, I'd love to have the distinction of being the first person to travel backward through time. But someone has to work the controls. And

I'm really the only one who knows how to operate this baby."

"Okay," said Jonathan in a shaky voice. As he sat down in the device he squeezed his eyes shut.

"You don't have to close your eyes," I said. "It's not like getting a shot at the doctor's office. It's not going to hurt."

"It better not," he said. "And I better come back in one piece — a *live* piece!"

"Have I ever killed you with one of my experiments?" I asked him.

"Not yet," he replied.

I turned on the power source and made a few final adjustments.

"Ready?"

"Ready."

"Okay, here we go."

I flipped the switch and engaged the main power drive.

Of course, I was glad it was Jonathan who was taking the risk and not me, but I certainly didn't expect what happened next. First a bright flash of green light exploded in my face and a shower of sparks flew out of the chamber. That was followed by a high-pitched whining noise and a dull thudding explosion.

"Alex! What was that noise?" Mom called from the garden.

I ran to my open window.

"Just rearranging the furniture a little!" I hollered and slammed my window shut.

Mom shook her head and went back to weeding her tulip bed.

Something had gone terribly wrong. When a foul-smelling cloud of purple smoke cleared, Jonathan was *gone*! For a moment I just stood there totally stunned.

Then I saw something moving below eye level. I looked down, and there in the bottom of the chamber was a baby.

"Holy protons!" I gasped. "It's him!"

A baby Jonathan, wearing nothing but his baseball cap, looked up at me and started bawling at the top of his lungs.

"WAAAAAH!"

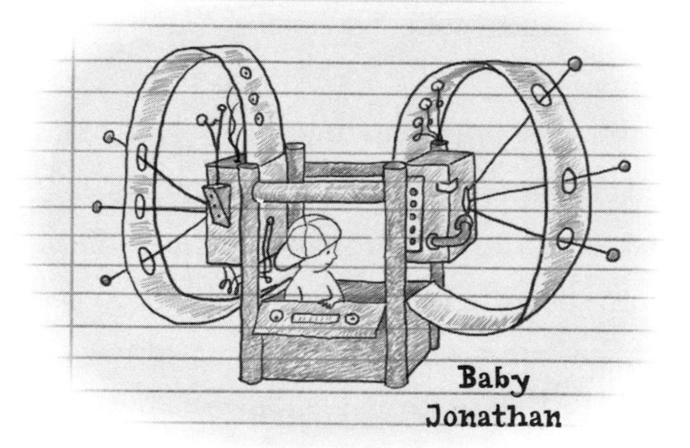

CHAPTER 6

Time Toddler

"Shut up!" I hissed. "Mom will hear you."

The word "Mom" made Baby Jonathan stop crying for a moment. I could see he was thinking about her. An instant later, when he realized she wasn't there, he started crying again — only louder this time.

So I picked him up.

"Shhh! Shhh! Shhh!" I hushed him.

But that just made him cry louder.

I was afraid Mom might walk in at any minute.

Luckily I remembered what Dad used to do when Mom wasn't around to nurse Jonathan. He would walk in circles and bounce him around like he was making a milkshake. So that's what I did. Once, twice, three times around my bedroom. Gradually he calmed down and began to coo.

I was planning on laying him on my bed so I could try to repair the time machine when I looked down and noticed that Jonathan was smiling up at me.

"Hi, Jonathan," I said and smiled back.

I was just thinking what a cute baby smile he had when I felt something warm in the palm of my left hand. Something warm and wet and — yellow!

"HE'S PEEING ON ME!" I cried as the puddle in my hand overflowed and splashed onto my sneakers. "He's peeing on me and my sneakers and smiling about it!"

I fought the impulse to drop the little creep and instead shoved him back in the chamber.

Then I wiped up the mess. Yuck! (Remind me *never* to have a baby.)

As I checked over the time converter and re-calibrated the time-flow distributor, Baby Jonathan started up with the screaming again. And this time he was louder than ever!

His screams were like ten rock-and-roll bands all playing at once. Just then I remembered the night Mom and Dad brought newborn Jonathan home from the hospital. It all came back to me in a flash. I had taken one look at the creep and known my life was ruined!

"Shut up!" I cried, readjusting the controls. "Just SHUT UP!"

Suddenly there was a knock on the door.

Oh, no! It's Mom! I thought.

"Who's there?" I called and quickly hid Jonathan's cap in my closet. I thought about hiding Jonathan in there, too, but there's no way that would muffle his banshee-like screams.

"It's me, Zoe," said the voice on the other side of the door. "I came over to get some of my things. Can I come in?"

"Yeah, yeah! Come in," I said, breathing a sigh of relief.

When Zoe opened the door and saw Jonathan her eyes lit up.

"Oh, what a cute baby!" she cried and rushed over to him.

"Shut the door!" I said, but she obviously didn't hear me, so I shut it myself.

Mr. Peace and Light

Zoe picked up Jonathan, and he started cooing again.

Go figure! One moment he's screaming his guts out and the next he's Mr. Peace and Light!

"What a *sweet* baby!" said Zoe. "I didn't know you did babysitting work."

"I don't," I said.

"Don't you think he should be wearing a diaper?" she asked.

"I don't have one," I replied.

Holding Jonathan in one arm, Zoe reached into her backpack and pulled out an orange gym towel.

"Somebody left you in charge of a baby without giving you diapers? Where are his clothes?" asked Zoe as she wrapped Jonathan in the towel.

"Look, you don't understand," I said. "That's not just some baby. That's Jonathan."

Zoe looked like someone had dropped a dead fly in her Coke.

"Jonathan?" she repeated.

"And that's a time machine," I said.

Zoe's eyes got that faraway look they sometimes get when she's thinking hard. "You're building a time machine to counteract the side effects of faster-than-light travel? Is that it?" she asked.

I nodded.

"Alex! That's amazing!" cried Zoe. "I came over to say goodbye, but now —"

"— you don't have to," I finished her thought.

"Unless you're still mad at me."

"Not as mad as I was yesterday," said Zoe. Then she looked down at Jonathan and the still-smoldering time machine. "What happened?"

"A fairly major glitch," I answered. "The creep was only supposed to go backward in time for minutes, not years!"

Jonathan grabbed Zoe's fingers and started sucking on her thumb.

"Gosh, he's cute!" she said.

"*Was* cute," I corrected her.

Zoe smiled down on him as if she were in a trance. I've seen babies have this effect on people before. I read somewhere that it has something to do with survival instincts.

"Yeow!" Zoe screamed and pulled her hand away. "The little creep bit me!"

When I looked at Jonathan I saw that he was wearing that little "I-got-you" grin that I had come to know so well.

Just then there was a knock on the door, and it opened right away. Only my mom does that.

"Oh, what a cute baby!" she cried.

This time it was Mom who thought Zoe was babysitting.

"Whose baby is it?" she asked.

"Ah …" Zoe needed a name quick, but my mind went blank. So I looked down and read the label on her backpack.

"It's the Wilson baby," I said.

Mom held out her arms to Jonathan.

"May I?" she asked Zoe.

Generally speaking, my mom can't keep her hands off babies. Whenever we go somewhere and there's a baby in the vicinity, it's only a matter of minutes before that baby is in Mom's arms and she's cooing and gooing and making faces at it.

But this was not like all those other times when Mom picked up someone else's baby. How could it be? It was *her* baby. It was *Jonathan*.

"Why, he looks ..." — all of a sudden Mom's voice got choked up, and a tear slipped out of her eye and rolled down her cheek — "just like Jonathan, doesn't he?" I've never seen her look so strange and sad.

"Nah," I said, my heart beating fast. "The creep had a much bigger nose."

"No, Alex," said Mom with a quiver in her voice. "This baby looks EXACTLY like your brother!" Then she buried her nose in his neck. "He even smells like Jonathan!" Mom actually looked a little scared. "Alex, where's your father?"

"I think he's in the garage working on the bookshelves," I replied. (Dad's been building bookshelves for as long as I can remember. He's been at it for so long that when he started he used rocks to pound in nails because hammers hadn't been invented yet.)

"Please call him, Alex," Mom insisted. "I don't want to holler out to the garage with this baby in my arms, but I want your father to see it."

"But, Mom, you know how Dad hates to be interrup —"

"ALEX!" Mom got that Godzilla look in her eye that says "OBEY! OBEY OR SUFFER DIRE CONSEQUENCES!"

Moving slowly, like someone shuffling down Death Row toward the electric chair, I walked over to the window and called out to the garage, "Dad!"

Momzilla

CHAPTER 7

Bad Timing

When Dad came into my bedroom he was holding a two-by-four in his hand and trailing a small cloud of sawdust.

"What is it?" he asked.

"I want you to see this Wilson baby," said Mom.

Dad rolled his eyes. "You called me away from the shelves to see ..."

Suddenly Dad's expression changed. It was like all the muscles in his face stopped working and the blood in his head drained down to his feet.

"If I didn't know it was impossible, I'd swear that baby is our Jonathan!" he exclaimed.

"I wanted you to see him," said Mom. "The resemblance is remarkable."

Jonathan really responded to the sight of Dad.

He held out his arms and bobbed up and down as if begging to be picked up.

"It's uncanny," said Dad as he set down the two-by-four and lifted Jonathan to his chest. "He could be Jonathan's twin brother. Don't you agree, Alex?"

"Wasn't Jonathan a lot fatter?" I asked.

"Alex wouldn't remember," said Mom. "He was too young."

"Where's Scout? He should see this," said Dad.

"Scout" used to be my nickname. But now it's what Dad calls Jonathan.

"Good idea," said Mom. "He's probably in his castle."

Zoe and I looked at each other. Jonathan was not in his castle. He was right in Mom's arms.

"Jonathan?" Dad went down the hall to Jonathan's room and came back a second later. "Nope. He's not in his castle. Now where could that kid be?"

Zoe whispered in my ear, "You'd better do something quick!"

"Yeah, but what?" I whispered back.

"What are you two conspiring about?" asked Mom.

"Ah … er …" Zoe gently scooped Jonathan out of Dad's arms. "I have to get Poocums back to the Wilsons'."

Conspiracy

Dad reluctantly let go of Jonathan.

"I guess Jonathan will have to see Poocums some other time," I said.

"Amazing," said Mom as Zoe made for the door. "That baby is so identical to our Jonathan ... I wonder if he has a similar birthmark on his bottom?"

I almost lost it at that point.

"No! No! Absolutely not. I'm sure he doesn't!" I exclaimed, knowing, of course, that he did.

"Let's find out," said Dad.

"That's ridiculous," I insisted. "The chances that this kid has the same mole in the same place are a billion to one."

"Even so, I'd like to check," insisted Dad, reaching for Jonathan.

Zoe walked right past him.

"Sorry, but I *really* must be going!" she said.

"I'll see you to the door," I offered and followed Zoe downstairs.

When we reached the front step Zoe turned to me. "So what do we do now?"

"Can you take him home for a while?" I asked.

"Are you crazy?" replied Zoe. "I can't just walk into my house with a baby. A stray cat maybe. Even a dog. But not a baby!"

"Okay! Okay!" I said. "Just take him down the front walk as if you're going home. But as soon as you're out of sight, cut across the Johnsons' lawn and double back to the side door. I'll wait for you there."

"Then what?"

"Then I'll put Jonathan in the time machine and *update* him."

"What if he cries and your parents hear?" asked Zoe.

I looked down at Jonathan. He was chewing on one of Zoe's buttons with a devilish look in his eyes.

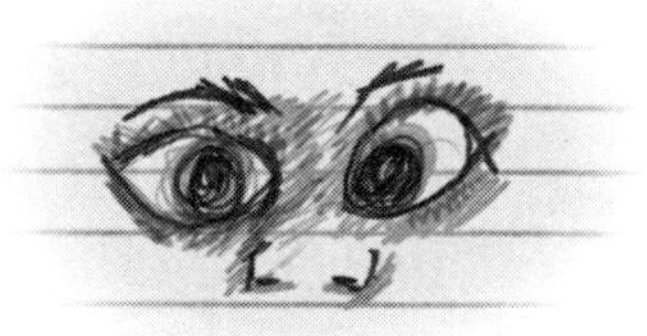

Devil Eyes

"Don't worry," I replied. "I'll think of something."

CHAPTER 8

Up against Time

After Zoe left I rummaged through the hall closet until I found the old boom box that nobody listens to anymore. I took it up to my room, plugged it in and tuned in the loudest rock-and-roll station I could find.

Boom Da Boom Da Boom Boom … "I love you Baby! I love you Baby!" Boom Da Boom Da Boom Boom …

The music was so loud it rattled the dishes in Mom's china cabinet. *Good,* I thought. *This will cover up any noises Jonathan might make.* Then I went downstairs and waited by the side door for Zoe to show up.

It seemed to take forever. By now Dad was back in the garage working on the shelves, and Mom was making dinner.

"Alex! Please turn down that music!" she hollered from the kitchen. "Music that loud is bad for your eardrums."

"Okay, Mom," I answered, ran upstairs again and turned it down just a tad.

Finally Zoe came to the door.

"Here he is," she said and shoved Jonathan into my arms.

"Aren't you coming in?" I asked. "I might need some help."

"What are you talking about?" whispered Zoe.

"I'm supposed to be taking Poocums back to the Wilsons', remember? If your parents come in and ..."

"Oh, yeah, right," I said.

Zoe was about to go, but I grabbed her wrist. "So if my time machine works are you going to be my copilot again?"

Zoe hesitated.

"Maybe," she said. "I have to think about it."

I was about to shout "*Think about it?!*" but I stopped myself.

"Okay, think about it," I said calmly. "Think about it and let me know."

"I will," she said and shut the door.

Jonathan had fallen asleep in my arms. When I got back to my room I rocked him back and forth a little to make sure he stayed that way and set him on the bed.

Then I turned to the time machine and made a few quick repairs. As I finished, Jonathan opened his eyes. I think he was expecting to see Zoe or Mom. When he saw me instead he immediately started bawling.

"Hold on, Poocums!" I set him down in the time chamber once more and turned up the rock and roll on the boom box. Then I calibrated the time markers to shift Jonathan forward in time to his present age. Finally I said a little prayer — "Please, somebody make this work!" — and flipped the power switch.

Seconds later, with no sparks, puffs of smoke or loud noises, Baby Jonathan disappeared. For a split second the chamber was empty. Then Jonathan reappeared. Not Baby Jonathan from the past but my rotten little six-year-old brother. Same dirty face and baseball cap sitting crookedly on his head.

I can't say I was actually glad to see the creep, but boy, was I relieved! The fact that I had successfully brought him back meant there was nothing wrong with my time machine that a few minor adjustments couldn't fix.

"Am I amazing or what?!" I cried.

"What?" shouted Jonathan. "Speak up. I can't hear you!"

"Never mind," I said and turned off the boom box.

"At last I can hear myself think," called Mom from downstairs. "Thank you!"

"So, how was it, Jonathan?" I asked.

Jonathan gave me a puzzled look.

"How was what?" he answered. "You mean those sparks? They didn't hurt."

"So … you don't remember being a baby again?"

Jonathan looked confused and then annoyed.

"Stop calling me a baby!" he demanded. "I'm six years old!"

Suddenly I realized that as far as Jonathan was concerned, he hadn't gone anywhere in time.

From his point of view the experiment hadn't even begun.

That's really weird, I thought. *According to my calculations, the subject should remember going back in time.*

Then I noticed the needle climbing toward maximum strength on the translocator gauge. I tapped the glass just to make sure it wasn't stuck. *Tap, tap, tap.* Still no change.

That's not right, I told myself and disengaged the power switch just to be on the safe side. But the power wouldn't turn off. The needle rose steadily into the red zone. *Uh-oh,* I thought. *This isn't good. This isn't good at all! I have to remove the power source.*

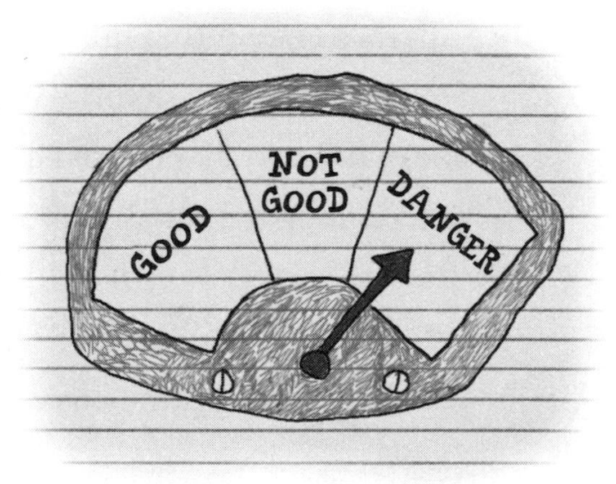

The power source was four AA batteries. I reached down, lifted a flap on the main control panel and popped them out. But the needle kept rising. *That's impossible,* I thought. *Unless ... somehow the electromagnetic field sequencer is transducing a positive feedback loop and generating its own power supply!*

All of a sudden I felt this strange pull toward the machine — as if I was an iron filing and the machine was a powerful magnet.

"You better get out of there," I said to Jonathan and offered him a hand.

"What's wrong?" he asked.

"Nothing serious," I lied. "Something electrogravitational must have gotten triggered. That's all."

I pulled on Jonathan's hand, but he didn't move.

"Jonathan, stop playing games," I said.

"I'm not playing games," he answered. "I'm stuck!"

"Cut it out!" I cried and pulled harder. He still wouldn't budge.

I grabbed Jonathan's other hand. But it was useless. It felt like he weighed a ton!

Then I saw something really terrifying. Jonathan started to swirl around. It was *sooo* freaky!

Everything in the room, including me, and the room itself started to spin in a clockwise rotation like a slow-moving tornado! At the center of what was now some kind of space/time vortex, the time machine began to warp and collapse in upon itself.

"I'm scared!" cried Jonathan. "What's happening?"

"I'm not really sure," I answered. "All I know is that we have to get out of this room!"

I turned toward the door, but it looked as if it was miles away! When I turned back I saw that the time machine had almost completely shrunk into itself.

Taking even a single step away from the vortex required a gargantuan effort. All my movements in the direction of escape slowed down as if I were stuck in a bowl of taffy.

My body was beginning to stretch out of shape, but Jonathan's already looked like a smear. I could make out his left arm and leg quite clearly. but the rest of him was just a smudge getting sucked down toward the dark void where the machine used to be.

I could hear the terror in my little brother's voice.

"Alex! Do something quick!" he cried. "It's like everything is getting sucked into that black hole!"

CHAPTER 9

The Black Hole

Black hole! Yes, that's exactly right, I thought. The time machine must have torn a gash in the fabric of space/time and was generating its own black hole!

If I didn't do something quick everything and I mean *everything* — Earth, the solar system and maybe even the whole galaxy — would get sucked into this hungry abyss.

"Heeelp!"

I could hear Jonathan's call for help, but I couldn't see him. The black hole had drawn him in completely.

As much as I loved the idea of my little brother disappearing forever into a bottomless abyss, I turned in the direction of his call for help and dove headfirst into the black hole.

It was like falling down a long, dark tunnel. Luckily I'd done some reading about black holes.

So I knew what I was dealing with.

Every black hole generates a gravitational field so strong even light particles — photons — can't escape its powers of attraction. That's why a black hole is black. No light can escape from it. The point where everything goes in and nothing goes out is called the event horizon. I knew I was there when I was engulfed in total darkness — a black so black it seemed impossible that light could ever shine again.

Headfirst into the Black Hole

Slowly the space between the individual atoms in my body stretched farther and farther apart. It was the strangest sensation — like being stretched from Earth to the moon!

I couldn't see Jonathan, but I could sense him near me in the void.

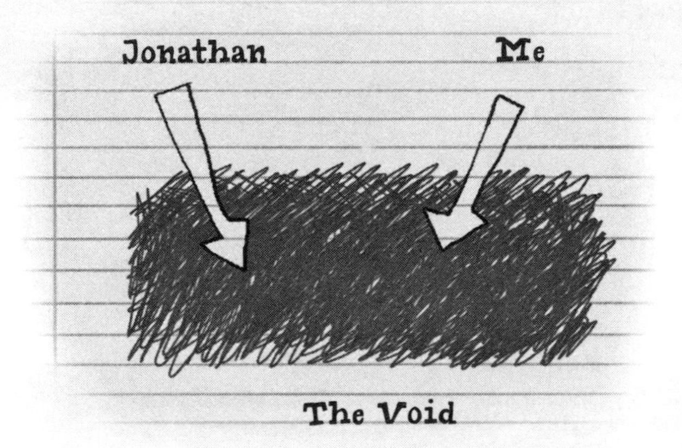

"Jonathan?" I called out. "Can you reach the machine?"

In this strange, dark nothingness, my words moved like worms from my mouth to Jonathan's ears. It was so freaky! Each word-worm had a different color and its own way of wiggling.

"Yeah, I think so," he replied.

"If we don't cut the feedback loop, the whole galaxy is going to collapse into my bedroom and disappear! So you'd better do exactly what I tell you!"

"*Really?* The whole galaxy into your bedroom!" he answered. "Wow! That's far out!"

"Jonathan!" I cried. "This is serious! Do exactly what I tell you to do!"

"Yeah, yeah, I hear you," he said with an extra-long blue worm that I took for a sigh.

The word-worms really started flying back and forth.

"Reach down into the workings of the machine and start pulling it apart!"

"You want me to *break* it?!"

"That's right," I said. "Wreck it! The whole thing."

"You won't get mad at me later?"

"Jonathan!" I shouted. "The fate of the entire galaxy is at stake! *Wreck it*!"

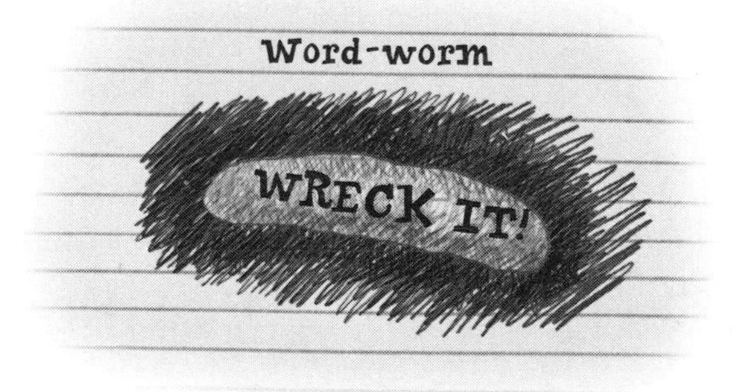

"Whatever you say, oh mighty one," said Jonathan in word-worms that were bright yellow.

As soon as he began ripping the time machine apart there was a brief flash of light. Instantly I felt a shift! The black hole's power source was diminishing.

Wooooooooooooopppaaaa ... It sounded like someone turning off a vacuum cleaner as huge as a cement truck.

"It's working!" I cried. "Keep pulling things apart!"

"It is?"

"Yeah, can't you feel it? The M-factor is reversing!"

"What?" yelled Jonathan.

"Never mind!" I said. "You did it! That's what counts."

I could already see the dim outline of Jonathan's face.

The danger was over. Now that the feedback loop was broken it was only a matter of minutes before the space/time coordinates of my bedroom returned to normal.

Slowly the black hole reversed itself and the time machine, totally wrecked, re-emerged onto my bedroom floor.

Now, not all my past experiments have been successful. For example, I once made a batch of disappearing ink that burned a hole clean through Mom's dining room table. (Boy, was she mad!) Another time I built a rocket booster for my bike that blew a six-foot hole in the garage door. But I had never built anything that nearly destroyed the galaxy before! I had never even come close.

Jonathan was lying on the floor beside me. Pieces of the time machine were scattered all around us. As I reached out to touch Jonathan to make sure he was okay, I noticed that my hands were shaking.

"Are you all right, Jonathan?"

Jonathan sat up and grinned.

"Yeah, I'm fine." He picked up several bits and pieces of wire and tattered cardboard. "But your time machine is a mess."

I kicked a piece of it with my foot. "Yeah, you did a good job of wrecking it."

"I guess you'll have to start all over with a new design," he said.

I was in some kind of shock. I sat there in a daze for a while before I could even attempt to respond. Had anyone ever come so close to destroying the entire universe?

"Start all over?" I said and hugged myself to make my hands stop shaking. "No way!"

CHAPTER 10

Time Goggles

The next day after school as I was going through my notes and designs, ripping out anything that related to time travel and throwing it in the trash, Jonathan burst through my door and flopped on the bed.

"I got an A in art today," he said, holding up a piece of paper. "I drew a paper clip climbing a mountain. Want to see?"

Needless to say I was not in the mood for a visit from the creep. I was not in the mood for a visit from anybody.

"No, I don't want to see a picture of a paper clip climbing a mountain," I said.

"How about this picture of Merlin and King Arthur on a picnic?" he said, holding up another sheet of paper. "I did this one yesterday."

"*No!*" I snapped. "I don't want to see any of your stupid pictures!"

"You sound grumpy," said Jonathan. "You going to throw me out?"

"It depends on how rotten you are," I said.

"*Me*, rotten?" he exclaimed. "You're the one who's rotten."

I didn't bother to reply. I just ripped out another page of formulas and threw it in the trash. My plan was to take them out in the backyard and burn them.

"If you want some help with the new Time Twister, I'm available," said Jonathan.

"I *told* you. There isn't going to be a new time machine!"

"Just show me the drawings, then," he said. "You must have drawings by now."

"Weren't you listening? There aren't going to be any more time machines. No formulas. No drawings. Nothing!"

Jonathan stared at me with a mixture of disbelief and shock. Either I wasn't the brother he knew me to be or I was lying to him. He wasn't sure which.

"Read my lips," I said. "No more time machines!"

"But why?" he asked. "I thought what we did yesterday was pretty neat."

"*Neat?!*" I exclaimed. "Almost destroying the entire planet, the solar system and all the stars and planets in our galaxy! You call that neat?"

"Yeah, it was just like in that movie we saw last week when Dr. Einstein's monster got loose."

"It wasn't Dr. Einstein's monster," I corrected him. "It was Dr. Frankenstein's monster."

"Oh, yeah, right," he said. "I get those two mixed up. But didn't Einstein create a monster too? Didn't he make the first atomic bomb?"

"No he didn't!" I snapped. "He published the formulas that made it possible for *other* scientists to make the bomb. And you know what? Some of them were just like you! They thought the bomb might cause a chain reaction that would incinerate the entire planet — but they tested it anyway!"

Jonathan's eyes lit up as if he were watching Earth explode like a giant firecracker.

Earthcracker

"Wow! That would have been one hubangous explosion!"

"Forget it," I said. "Talking to you is like talking to bubble wrap."

Jonathan stood up on my bed and shouted, "Stop saying stuff like that! Stop it!"

"Nobody invited you in here," I replied. "If you don't like what you're hearing get out!"

Jonathan jumped off my bed and headed for the door.

"I'm going to talk to Merlin about this," he said. "He'll know what to do!"

"Fine. You do that," I said. "Just close my door on the way out! And while you're at it, ask King Arthur to take you away on a long quest!"

I was glad to get rid of the creep and be alone. I had never given up on a scientific challenge before, and I did not like how it felt. Sure, I had some new ideas to try out, improvements on my old design. One of them might even be the one that would make it safe. But I didn't even write them down. I didn't *dare* attempt another prototype. What had happened yesterday might not have scared Jonathan, but it had *terrified* me. What if I tried the wrong idea first? What if I created another black hole — a bigger, hungrier, more vicious void! And what if I couldn't stop it? What if I ended up destroying more than the Milky Way? What if I destroyed the entire universe? I'm a scientist. Not a *mad* scientist. I did not want to go down in history as the scientist who totally obliterated history!

About twenty minutes later Jonathan pushed open my door.

"I'm back!" he announced.

"Yeah, so?" I said, not looking up from my notebook. "Any other bad news?"

I was still at my desk facing away from the door.

"Turn around," he said.

"Go away. I'm busy," I told him.

"No. Turn around!" he insisted.

So I did — sometimes it's just not worth arguing with the creep. It's like trying to argue with the wind. In the long run it's just easier to give in.

When I turned around I saw that Jonathan was wearing an unusual contraption on his head. It was made of two toilet paper rolls and paper clips duct taped to an old pair of glasses.

"Ask me what these are," begged Jonathan.

"I have a feeling you're going to tell me anyway," I replied.

"They're time goggles," said the creep. "Merlin showed me how to make them."

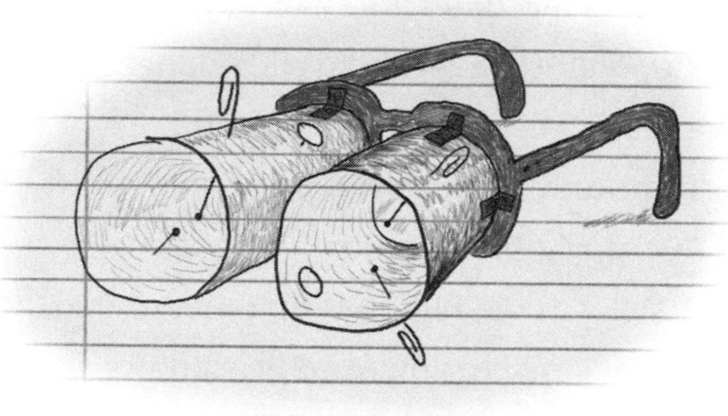

Time Goggles

"Huh," I replied and turned back to the notebook on my desk. "And now I guess you're going to tell me what time goggles are."

"Yep, you got it!" continued Jonathan. "Merlin says time travel is invented in the year 2264. He says that in the future lots of people have time machines.

In the future they'll sell time machines at the check-out counters in drug stores and grocery stores — only most food won't be sold in stores anymore because it'll come through the TV. Anyway, in the future, time machines are small and they're cheap. But they're not like MP3 players. You need to pass a test and get a license to operate one."

I was only half listening.

"Go on," I said.

"Well, I asked Merlin if that meant there were time travelers here now. And he said yes, they're everywhere, like tourists."

"Time tourists?" I looked up.

"That's right," he replied. "And some times are more popular than others."

"How about our time?" I asked. "I bet nobody wants to come here."

"Actually, Merlin said our century is a very popular time-tourist attraction."

I guess I should have been glad for the distraction Jonathan was providing. But I wasn't. I just wanted him to go away so I could get back to being miserable.

"So how come we don't see any of these time tourists?" I asked.

"That's just what I asked Merlin," said Jonathan. "And you know what he said?"

"Because they're invisible?" I asked.

Jonathan walked over to me and stood on his tippy toes.

"Because they're invisible!" he whispered in my ear.

"Uh-huh, I get it," I said, my attention rising to the level of mildly interested. "Because if they weren't invisible they'd create time paradoxes?"

"Right! That's just what Merlin said!" exclaimed Jonathan. "Were you listening at the door when I was talking to him?"

"Don't be ridiculous." I rolled my eyes. "What else did Merlin say?"

"Lots of things," answered Jonathan. "But mostly he told me how to build these." He pointed to the contraption on his face.

I had to give Jonathan credit for having a good imagination. After all, it was the same imagination he had been using to torment me all these years.

"And what do time goggles do?" I asked skeptically.

"They make invisible time travelers visible," said Jonathan. "Want to try them on?"

Just then Mom hollered from downstairs, "Alex, you have a visitor!"

"Okay, I'll be right there," I answered.

As I got up from my chair Jonathan took off his time goggles and held them out to me.

"Just try them," he said. "You'll see."

CHAPTER 11

Time Zone

When I came downstairs I saw Zoe standing beside Mom's prize African violet.

"I came over to see how you were doing," Zoe whispered.

My mom was in the next room, and I didn't want her to hear what we were saying.

"Let's sit outside," I said and gently shoved Zoe out the front door and onto the porch. As I went to close the door Jonathan squeezed out and joined us.

"Do you always have to follow me around?" I snapped.

"Just try the goggles," he said and shoved them in my face.

When Zoe saw Jonathan she greeted him with a pat on the head and a "Hi, Poocums."

Jonathan scowled. "*What* did you call me?"

"Never mind," said Zoe with a smile. "So Jonathan's back. Does that mean our time machine is working?"

"Alex gave up on it," said Jonathan.

Zoe looked at me in utter disbelief. She knew me well enough to know that giving up on an invention is not like me at all.

"Yeah, Jonathan's right," I said and told her the whole story of how I had almost destroyed the entire universe.

"But are you sure there isn't some safe way ... ?" she began.

"No." I shook my head. "If there was, believe me, I'd try it."

Jonathan tugged at my shirt.

"I'm telling you, these goggles are the answer. Just try 'em."

"Excuse me, Zoe," I said and turned to the creep.

"Look, you're being a real pest right now. Either go away or SHUT UP! Okay?"

"I just want you to try on these goggles," said Jonathan. "Just once."

Zoe tapped me on the shoulder. "Alex, can't you be just a *little* nice to him?"

"Sure I can," I said, unable to hide the exasperation in my voice. "I can be very nice to him." I turned to Jonathan. "Tell you what I'm going to do," I said. "I'll make a bargain with you, Jonathan. I'll try on the goggles, and then you'll go away and leave Zoe and me alone. Is that a deal?"

Jonathan handed me the goggles with a big grin. "Deal!"

I took off my own glasses and slid them into my shirt pocket. Then I put on the goggles. The fit was a little snug but not too tight. Without my regular glasses everything looked a little blurry. Other than that I didn't see anything unusual.

"Okay, I've tried on the glasses," I said starting to take them off. "And everything looks the same."

"Wait a minute," said Jonathan. "You didn't really look."

I was about to hand them back to Jonathan when Zoe gave me a dirty look. So I decided to humor the creep a tad longer.

"All right, I'm looking," I said.

"Tell me what you see," said Jonathan.

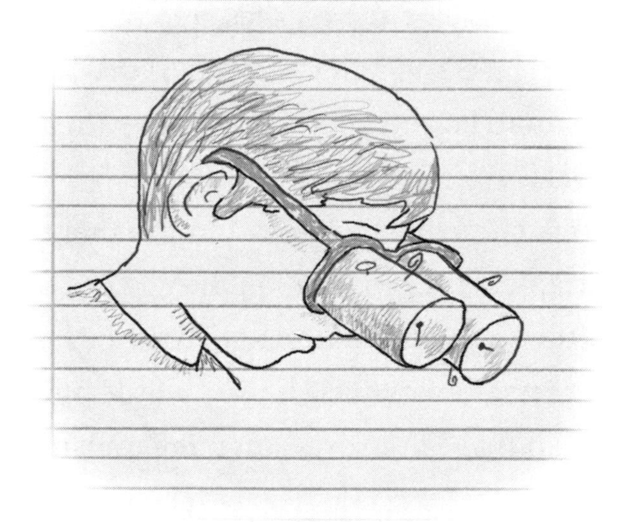

"The front lawn, the sidewalk, the street, some people ..." I answered.

"How many people do you see?" asked Jonathan.

"Four — one lady walking her dog, two people in a car and the man leaning against that tree over there."

"What man?" said Zoe.

"That man," I said, pointing to the guy by the tree. "He's totally bald, about thirty years old and wearing a light-blue jumpsuit."

"There's no one standing over there," said Zoe.

"What are you talking about?" I said.

"You see!" said Jonathan. "They're working. Now lift the goggles."

I pushed the goggles up on my forehead, and suddenly the man disappeared.

I lowered the goggles and looked again. He was back!

"Now that's ... That's really something ..." I said, raising and lowering the goggles. Every time I looked without them the man disappeared. Every time I looked with them he was standing right there.

"Wow!" I took off the glasses and examined them. "Jonathan! How …?" I couldn't find the words to express my surprise. I knew Jonathan shared some of my scientific genes. But these goggles were truly amazing!

"I told you. Merlin showed me."

"No, *really,*" I said, touching one of the paper clips. "How did you know — ?"

"Careful," said Jonathan. "If you jiggle one of those paper clips even an eighth of an inch it won't work. Merlin wrote down the measurements, and I used a ruler to get them right."

"Can I try?" asked Zoe.

"Sure," I said and handed her the goggles.

"Oh my gosh!" she cried. "This is scary. Who *is* that guy?"

"He's a time traveler," said Jonathan. "Merlin says there are lots of them around all the time, only we can't see them because they don't want us to."

"Incredible!" I gasped. "But it does make perfect sense when you think about it."

"Maybe it makes perfect sense to you," said Zoe. "But I don't get it."

I did my best to explain. "Time travel hasn't been invented yet, right? But someday it will be. When that happens, time travelers will go forward and backward in time but they won't be allowed to make any changes. If they did, it might upset things."

"What things?" asked Zoe.

"Chains of events," I replied. "For example, what if you went back in time and accidentally caused the death of your grandfather?"

"Then you wouldn't get born," answered Zoe.

"But if you weren't born, then you couldn't cause the death of your grandfather," said Jonathan.

"Right," I said. "It's a time paradox. If people interacted with time travelers it would cause lots of time paradoxes. And that would lead to total time chaos. The inventors of time travel must have realized this and made laws forcing time travelers to remain invisible."

"But we're seeing them," said Jonathan. "Isn't that cool?"

"Way cool, Jonathan," I said. "Way cool."

And risky, too, I thought to myself. But I didn't say so out loud because I didn't want to freak out Zoe.

Just then Zoe nudged me and said, "Hey, the man in the blue jumpsuit just reached into his bag and took out something that looks like a cell phone. Now he's flipping it open and pushing some buttons. I think he's making a call!"

I asked for a turn with the goggles and took a look. "Maybe, maybe not," I said.

Suddenly the guy disappeared.

"That was no cell phone!" I exclaimed. "That was his time machine."

I handed the goggles back to Zoe. "See, he's gone."

"So where did he go?" asked Zoe.

"Who knows?" I answered. "Could be a hundred years into the past or ten days into the future. When you have a time machine you can go anywhere anytime you want."

"Too bad we can't follow him," said Jonathan. "Then we could *borrow* his time machine. Or at least take it apart and see how it works."

For once I was beginning to appreciate Jonathan's devious little mind.

“Good idea, Jonathan,” I said. Then I turned to Zoe. “Got your camera?”

“Of course.” Zoe reached into her backpack and pulled out her point-and-shoot. “You know me. I never leave home without it.”

“Good,” I said. “Is it charged up?”

She checked the battery.

“Almost full.”

“Also good,” I said. “Now here’s the plan …”

CHAPTER 12

Time Tourists

The first thing we did was go up to my room and make two additional pairs of time goggles — one for me and one for Zoe. The hard part was finding old glasses that fit. After that the rest was easy. In twenty minutes we were ready to go out hunting for time travelers.

I'm sure the three of us looked kind of goofy walking down the street wearing time goggles. Passersby must have thought, *What weird things these kids wear nowadays!*

We didn't spot any time travelers on MacMearson Street or Doolittle Street. But as we got closer to downtown — Holland and 18th Street — they started to show up all over the place.

The best way to spot them was to keep raising your time goggles. Otherwise you might just think they were ordinary people. Well, actually, you'd only miss a few of them that way. Some time travelers appeared more or less ordinary. Unless you looked closely you wouldn't necessarily notice little things like the fact that there were no wrinkles in their clothes or that their wristwatches were actually tiny computers.

Most time travelers, however, stuck out like sore thumbs. Many of them didn't even walk in the usual way. Instead they rolled along on tiny wheels that appeared to take the place of their feet.

Others wore strange headbands that appeared to give them the power to see 360 degrees.

Some of the time travelers seemed to be traveling purposefully from one place to another like business people on their way to important meetings. Others wandered around like tourists looking at everything. Perfectly normal objects like bicycles and baby carriages seemed to fascinate them. I saw one time traveler looking at a fire hydrant with a magnifying glass. The expression on his face was so serious. He reminded me of an archaeologist studying an ancient artifact.

Near Wipole's Drug Store on the corner of Main and 4th, we spotted a couple of time tourists with a large robotic dog walking beside them. The woman was very tall and wore metallic clothing. Or maybe part of her was actually made of some kind of shiny copper metal — I couldn't tell for sure. The oddest thing about her was her head. It was almost transparent. You could see her eyeballs and the veins all around them. You could see the teeth inside her cheeks and the brain inside her skull.

"Oooh, that's so gross!" said Jonathan.

"Do you think it could be some kind of futuristic fashion statement?" wondered Zoe.

The man was similarly dressed but did not have any transparent body parts. He did, however, have a large Swiss army knife contraption where his right hand should have been.

Their dog looked like a completely normal golden retriever, but I knew it was a robot because I saw it do something no ordinary dog could do. The man was eating an apple. When he finished taking the last bite he said "command 42" and a tiny door opened up on top of the dog's head. Bright yellow flames shot out. The man dropped the apple core into the opening. There was a puff of gray smoke. Then the door shut. Obviously only a robotic dog could do something like that!

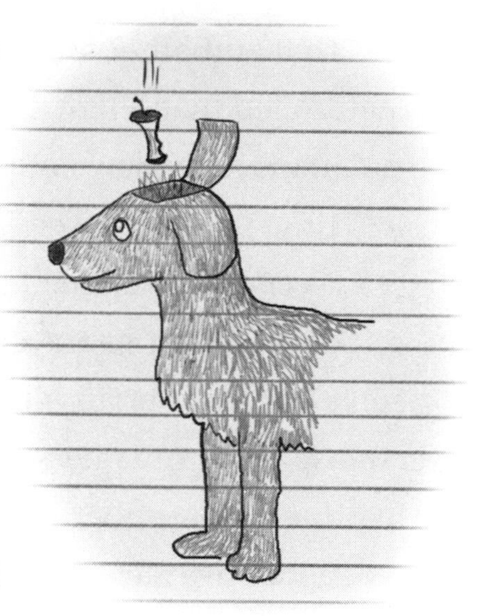

Robo-dog

We saw lots of time travelers on guided tours in groups as large as a dozen or more. They laughed and talked loudly among themselves. But nobody besides us appeared to see or hear them.

Jonathan got very excited when we saw a time traveler who had apparently mastered the art of levitation. "Hey, let's talk to that guy and ask him how he does it!"

"Absolutely not!" I insisted. "We don't want any time travelers knowing we see them."

"Time paradoxes?" asked Zoe.

"That and other reasons," I said. "If time travel is controlled then there must be regulations. And regulations mean law enforcement."

"Time police?" asked Jonathan.

"Precisely," I replied.

Some of the time travelers we saw weren't whole people at all, just brains floating in transparent containers. They drifted down the street about five feet above the sidewalk emitting strange high-pitched beeps that sounded a lot like dolphin noises.

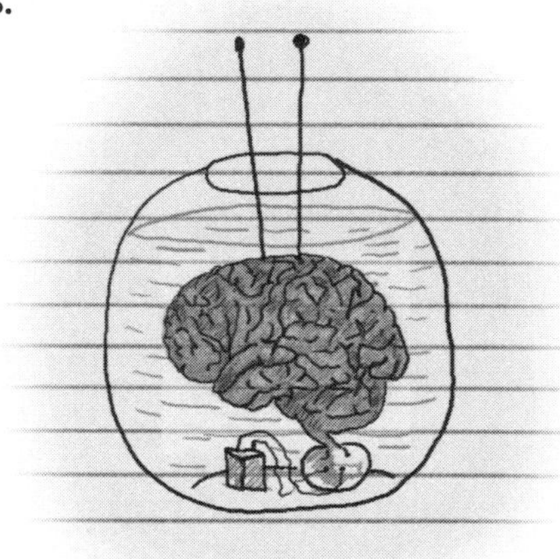

"What in the world are those?" exclaimed Zoe.

I didn't know for sure, but I had a theory. "I think they're people from the really far-off future who know how to separate their brains from their bodies."

"Spooky," said Jonathan.

"Spooky but fascinating," said Zoe. "I'd love to know how it's done."

We must have wandered around town for more than an hour just gawking at some of the most extraordinary people you can imagine. But I was doing something more than sight-seeing. I was also looking for a ripe opportunity to borrow a time machine.

Finally, I saw exactly what I was looking for. We were just crossing the park near the center of town when I glimpsed a time traveler sound asleep under a tall oak tree. It was a young woman wearing what could only be described as a wedding dress of the future. It was white and frilly with long flickering strands of tiny electric lights built into its puffy, fluffy fabric.

I guess some bizarre traditions like impractical wedding dresses never change, I thought. *They just get more bizarre.*

"Look at that!" said Jonathan. "I wonder why she's lying there all by herself instead of getting married?"

"Maybe she was about to get married and got cold feet so she escaped into another time," guessed Zoe. "Do you have a theory, Alex?"

"No, but I'm very interested in her handbag," I answered.

Next to the woman lay a white bag, which, except for its color, was more or less the same size and shape as the bag that belonged to the guy in the blue jumpsuit.

"Her time machine has got to be in there," I said and slowly moved toward the bride and her bag.

"Wait a minute," said Zoe. "You can't just steal someone's bag! That's against the law."

"Shhh! Not so loud," I said. "You'll wake her."

"But Alex —"

"Don't worry. I'm not going to steal anything. Get your camera ready. I just want to take a picture of a working time machine so I can study it and build a safe version of my own."

By now we were just a few feet away from the woman. I was so close I could see her stomach rise and fall as she breathed. Slowly I reached forward and wrapped my fingers around the strap of her bag.

Holding the bag with one hand, I tried to lift the silver clasp. Nothing happened. So I turned the clasp. Still nothing. I twisted and pulled. Still nothing.

Then Zoe bent forward and whispered into the clasp, "Open!"

Instantly, the hinge of the bag swung wide.

Zoe shrugged with a sheepish grin. "It's the future, right?"

Inside were several strange objects, any of which could have been the woman's time machine.

If only I had been closer to the guy in the blue jumpsuit, I thought. *I might have gotten a better look at his time machine.*

I started fumbling through the bag. “Is that a time machine or a makeup kit?” I asked myself. “And what the heck is that thing?”

“Let me see,” said Jonathan as he pushed forward.

“Shut up and stay back!” I whispered, giving him a shove.

But it was too late.

The woman’s eyelids fluttered open, and she stared at me with the most peculiar expression of shock and disbelief. Somehow she must have known I wasn’t a fellow time traveler. I wasn’t supposed to be able to see her, but it was obvious that I could.

“Who are you?” she asked in a trembling voice.

Instead of answering, I panicked.

I scooped up her bag and slung it over my shoulder.

“Run everyone!” I shouted. “Run as fast as you can!”

CHAPTER 13

A Matter of Time

It was a lucky thing the time traveler was wearing that frilly wedding gown. By the time she managed to stand up we were halfway out of the park. When I looked back to make sure Jonathan wasn't lagging too far behind I didn't see him. But that was only because he was way ahead of us! I've never seen anyone run so fast on such short legs. The bride was pursuing us as quickly as she could, but there was no way she was going to catch us in that dress.

"Alex, this is crazy!" cried Zoe.

"I know!" I said and grabbed her hand.

By the time we got to my house Zoe was panting heavily and my side hurt so badly I could hardly stand up straight. Only Jonathan wasn't totally out of breath.

"Now what?" he asked as Zoe and I dragged

ourselves up the walk to the front step.

Just then Mom opened the front door.

"Oh, good, you're home," she said. "Your Dad is taking a nap in the den and I'm going downtown for a moment to pick up some whipping cream for the dessert I'm making for tonight. Please play quietly and try not to disturb your father."

Disturb Dad? She had to be kidding. When Dad takes a nap, nothing short of heavy explosives can wake him.

"Sure, Mom," I said.

Mom grabbed the van keys from the hall table and was about to leave when she noticed the time goggles.

"And what, may I ask, are those contraptions?"

"These ... ah ... err ... these are time goggles," I said. "When you wear them you can see time travelers."

"Ah ... so the game is time travel today, is it?"

she said smiling. "Well, carry on."

As soon as Mom left we ran upstairs to my bedroom where we quickly dumped the contents of the white bag on my bed.

It was the weirdest collection of stuff I ever saw. Hardly any of it was identifiable.

"One of these things is a time machine," I said. "The problem is, which one?"

Jonathan immediately made a grab for every item on my bed as if they were presents under a Christmas tree. But I pushed him away.

"Let me see!" he protested. "You wouldn't have any of this stuff if it wasn't for my time goggles!"

"Don't touch anything!" I warned.

"Why the heck not?" he whined.

"Because one of these items could be a security device."

"You mean like a mace container or a stun gun?" asked Zoe.

"Precisely," I said. "For example, that thing" — I pointed to a red plastic cylinder — "could be the future version of a hand gun."

"Or a place to put snacks!" said Jonathan.

"Don't worry, we'll let you know if we find any futuristic snacks," I replied.

"So you don't want me touching anything, do you?" asked Jonathan.

"That's right," I said. "Zoe and I will check out this stuff."

"I thought so," Jonathan pouted. "You big guys get to do everything, and all I get to do is watch."

This was the way the old whiny, nasty Jonathan talked. I knew his "good kid" routine couldn't last long. Rotten Jonathan was always lurking just beneath the surface. Sooner or later he'd be back. It was only a matter of time.

"Actually, there's something *very* important we need you to do right now," said Zoe.

Jonathan perked up.

"What's that?" he asked.

"You can put on your time goggles and keep an eye out for that woman in the park just in case she follows us here."

"Sure thing!" Jonathan gladly put on his goggles and plopped himself down on my window seat.

"You see?" Zoe whispered to me. "He just wants to help."

Now that Jonathan was out of our way, Zoe and I got down to the serious business of finding the time machine. First we counted what was in the bag — seventeen items in all. Then we made two piles: pile one — likely stuff, and pile two —

unlikely stuff. We decided this mostly according to size. Really large items and really small items went in the unlikely pile.

In the end we had ten items in the unlikely pile and seven items in the likely pile.

"Okay. Let's take turns," I suggested. "First you pick one, then I'll pick."

"Okay." Zoe lifted the red cylinder off the bed and handed it to me. "How about this?"

"Hmm," I said hefting the cylinder in my hand. "It seems rather light to be a time machine. But here goes."

I twisted the cylinder open. Inside was an intricate panel of buttons, knobs, tubes and nozzles.

"That looks promising," said Zoe. "Maybe we hit it on our first try."

"Nobody's coming so far," reported Jonathan.

"Did you check the other windows?" asked Zoe.

"Right!" Jonathan slapped his hand with a fist. "I forgot about that!"

Jonathan started running from room to room checking out the windows to see if we had been followed.

With Jonathan out of the way we were free to get back to work on the cylinder.

"I think that red button is the power button," I said. "I'm going to push it."

"Hold it away from your body and point it at the wall," said Zoe. "Just in case."

"Good idea," I replied and pushed the red button.

The cylinder made a gurgling noise and grew warm in my hand. Then a thin silver rod, something like a tiny vacuum cleaner hose, shot out of one end.

"What the heck is that?" gasped Zoe.

"I guess the only way to find out is to push another button," I said.

"Careful," she warned.

Immediately water started spurting out one end of the hose and splashing both of us.

"Turn it off!" Zoe cried.

I tried turning one of the small blue knobs, but that only made the water hotter.

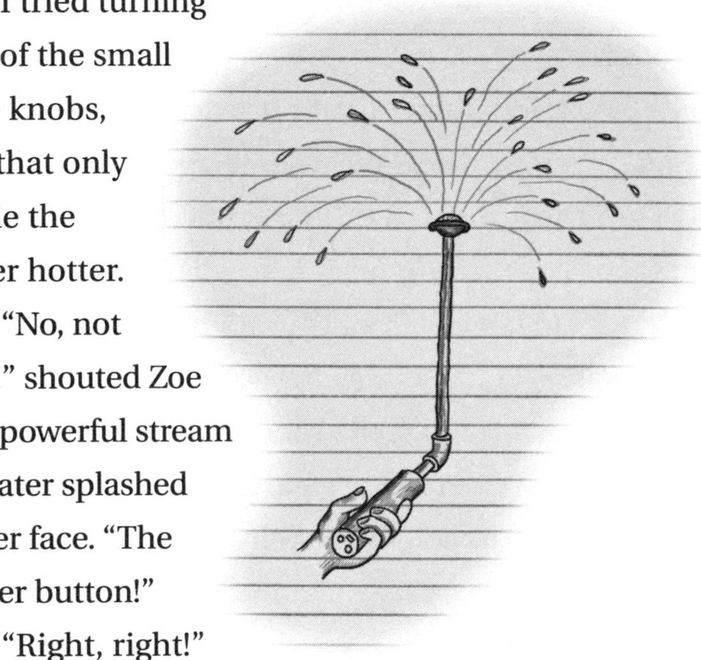

"No, not that!" shouted Zoe as a powerful stream of water splashed in her face. "The power button!"

"Right, right!" I said and pushed the red power button.

The huge gush of water abruptly stopped, and the long tube retracted into the red cylinder.

"I believe we just experienced a portable shower," said Zoe as she wiped her face on the edge of my bed covers.

“I guess in the future every well-equipped handbag will have one,” I commented.

It was such an absurd situation both of us burst out laughing.

“I wonder where all that water came from?” mused Zoe. “There’s no way that much water could fit in that little cylinder.”

“There must be some way of compressing it,” I said. “Or maybe it was teleported from another location.”

I lifted another object from the pile and handed it to Zoe. This one was egg shaped and lavender in color.

“Maybe this one is our time machine,” she said and flipped open the device.

Instantly a thin red laser shot across the room and a booming voice rang out, “AIM DEVICE AND FIRE ON COMMAND!”

CHAPTER 14

Time Loop

"It's some kind of weapon!" cried Zoe, dropping the lavender egg onto the bed. The device bounced once and landed near pile one.

"Holy Cosmic Cow!" I cried as the laser shot out across the room and made a wobbly red dot on my bureau.

Luckily the device had not been triggered. I gingerly reached down and was about to pick it up when Zoe cried, "Wait! What are you going to do?"

"Close it so it turns off," I said.

Just then Jonathan ran into the room.

"No sign of the lady so far," he reported. Then the laser weapon caught his eye. "Hey, what's that?"

Before I could say anything he scooped it up off the bed.

“Jonathan, no!” I cried. “That’s dangerous. Put it *down*!”

“Aw! You’re no fun!” he replied. “Let me just push a few of these buttons first.”

“Please, Jonathan, don’t!” insisted Zoe.

But it was too late. The red laser dot swung around the room and landed on Zoe.

Zaaaaaaaaooooooom!

A baseball-sized sphere of blue light slid down the pencil-thin laser beam and slammed Zoe in the stomach!

FoooouUM! It lifted her up off the floor and dropped her against the wall.

"RELOAD AND FIRE ON COMMAND," said the voice.

Horrified at what he had done, Jonathan immediately dropped the device, which closed as it fell.

"Gosh, I'm sorry!" he cried.

"Zoe!" I pushed Jonathan out of the way and leapt to her side.

Zoe was lying on the floor holding her stomach and trying to sit up.

"Are you okay?"

"I … I … can't … breathe," Zoe coughed as she struggled to get more air in her lungs.

I turned to Jonathan with murder in my heart.

"Now look what you did!" I shouted.

"I didn't mean to!" he protested. "I was just —"

"Of course you never *mean* to," I snapped. "But you always mess up. Don't you? Ever wonder why? Probably not. So I'll tell you why! Because you're a curse! That's right. A curse the universe put on me to pay for all my great talents!"

"Hey, Alex … take … it easy." Zoe's ability to breathe was gradually returning. "It was … just an accident. That's all." Then she turned to the creep. "I'm all right, Jonathan. Get back to your post, okay?"

Jonathan began to leave, but at the door he stopped. "I didn't mean to … Honestly, I didn't mean to …"

Zoe struggled to stand up.

"It's okay," she said, giving him a weak smile. "Now go do your job and let us do ours."

"Okay," said Jonathan and he disappeared down the hall.

I picked up the lavender egg and gently set it in the pile of rejects. "It's a darn good thing that device wasn't calibrated to deliver a lethal dose!" I said.

I got Zoe a glass of water. She took a sip and said, "Come on, we better get back to work."

"Are you sure you're okay?" I asked.

"Okay enough," she replied.

The next item we examined turned out to be a compressed food survival kit complete with fancy meals including a pill-sized turkey dinner with cranberry sauce and all the fixings. All you had to do was drop the pill in water and it expanded into a hot dinner. (I tasted some. It was great!)

Then we came across a miniature beauty parlor with options for shampooing and hair drying plus units for nail painting and foot massage. (Zoe wanted to try that one, but I convinced her there wasn't time.)

There were lots of fascinating items in that handbag, but one stuck out in particular. It was just a four-inch plastic cube, one side of which was translucent so we could see its inner workings.

"I think I know what this is and how it works," I said to Zoe and popped open its lid. I took a pencil from my desk and dropped it into the cube.

Instantly the pencil disappeared.

"Yep, I was right. It's a portable disposal unit," I declared and went to my bookshelf. There in my stack of scientific notebooks I found one entitled "New Concepts." I opened it, and my fingers instantly located the correct page of diagrams and schematics that explained how the cube actually functioned.

"So where's the pencil now?" asked Zoe.

"Somewhere in another world," I answered.

"By poking a tiny wormhole in the fabric of space/time this device creates a disposal chute into another dimension."

"It looks so much like your drawings. Do you think it's possible someone in the future based this unit on your sketch?"

"I wouldn't be surprised if that's exactly what happened," I said. "After all, I *am* the world's greatest supergenius. It's only logical to expect that the future will be crammed full of my inventions!"

It wasn't until we got to almost the bottom of the pile that we found what we were looking for.

"This looks promising," said Zoe, holding up a tan, triangular-shaped object that opened like a cell phone.

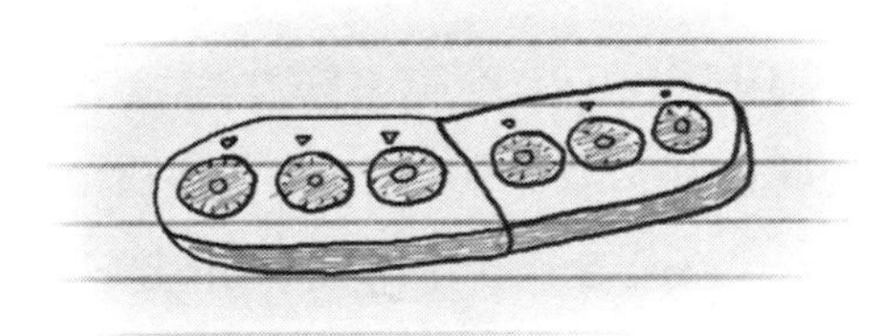

The interior of the device contained six transparent dials, all of which were covered in numbers.

"What do you think?" she asked.

"Promising," I said and gave the device a closer inspection. I noticed that each dial was marked by a different increment of time: "Years," "Months," "Days," "Hours," "Minutes" and "Seconds."

"This has to be it!" I exclaimed and reached for the "Seconds" dial.

"Wait," said Zoe.

When I looked up I saw her biting her lip.

"If it *is* the time machine and you turn the wrong dial we could disappear into another century," she said.

"That's a chance we'll have to take," I replied and turned the dial counter-clockwise ten notches.

Instantly, both of us (I guess because Zoe was touching my shoulder) slipped into a mini time warp. Time stopped going forward in the usual way. Instead we found ourselves back in time — precisely ten seconds ago.

The only way I can think of to describe the experience is to say it was like being *inside* an instant replay. There I was again opening the device and saying the exact same words I had said before:

"This has to be it!"

"Wait," said Zoe.

Again I saw her biting her lip and saying, "If it *is* the time machine and you turn the wrong dial ..." and so on, and so forth.

We were reliving the past ten seconds for a second time until abruptly the experience ended. We both just stared at each other dumbfounded. Then we grinned at exactly the same time and said, "We found it!"

"Now what?" asked Zoe.

“Now I take this thing apart and see what makes it tick,” I answered.

There were some extremely tiny screws on the back of the device. Luckily I had a screwdriver small enough to fit them. In a matter of seconds I had the back cover off and was analyzing how the device worked.

But before I could get very far, Jonathan, still wearing his time goggles, rushed into the room.

“They’re here!” he shouted.

“Who’s here?” asked Zoe.

“I don’t know!” cried Jonathan. “But they’re definitely from the future, and they’ve got the house surrounded!”

CHAPTER 15

The Time Police

I slipped on my goggles and ran from one window to the next. Everywhere I looked I saw the same thing: shiny black orbs about two feet in diameter converging on the house.

There were two by the front walk, one in Mom's hydrangea bushes, three by the garage — and at least *ten* in the backyard! All of them hovered about four feet above the ground as they moved steadily toward their destination — us!

Oddly enough in the midst of this threat my very first thought was, *I've seen these things before.* I knew it was a completely irrational thought, but their odd, facial-like markings and peculiar antenna arrangement looked hauntingly familiar.

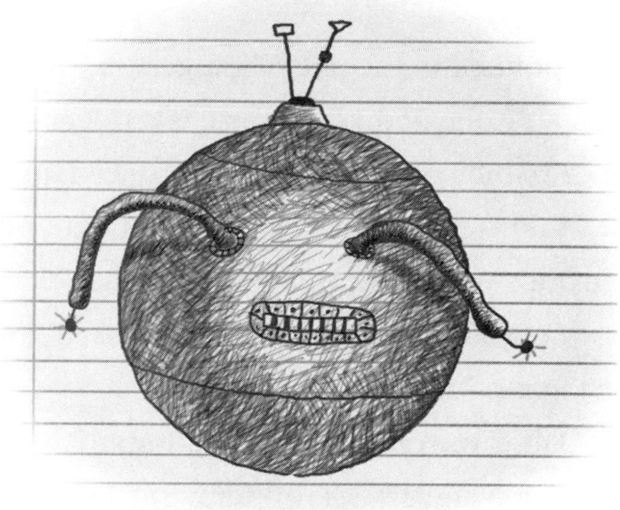

Time Police

“Let me see!” Zoe tried on her goggles.

“They’re all so similar. It’s hard to tell one from the other,” she said. “I wonder if they’re robots?”

“Yeah! I think you’re right, Zoe,” I said. “It makes perfect sense to use robots for time police. Less chance of time paradoxes that way.”

“How did they find us?” asked Jonathan. “That lady never showed up.”

I pointed to the pile of gadgets on the bed. "Probably one of these items has a tracer in it."

"Are they going to arrest us?" asked Jonathan.

"I don't know," I answered. "But one thing's for sure: they want their time machine back!"

"So what are we going to do?" asked Zoe. "We can't just —"

"Don't worry, I have a plan. Jonathan, run to your castle and ask Merlin for some advice!"

Jonathan puffed up with pride. "Right!" he cried and flew out of the room as if his feet were on fire.

Zoe eyed me skeptically. "That's your plan — ask Merlin for advice?"

"That was just a ploy to get Jonathan out of the way," I said and grabbed the time machine from the bed. "We're taking this time machine and getting out of here."

I ran to Star Jumper and opened the hatch.

"But that's stealing!" protested Zoe.

"No it isn't," I said. "If we escape now, that will give me time to duplicate it. Then I can use *my* time machine to go back in time and return *this* one to the woman in the park!"

Zoe thought for a moment, mulling over my plan — my whole plan.

"Then you're not going to take Jonathan with us like you promised him. Are you?" she said flatly.

"Of course not," I replied. "You just experienced at first hand how dangerous that little pest can be."

"Everyone messes up once in a while," said Zoe. "He's just a little kid."

I walked over to the window. Even more time police had gathered by now. There must have been three dozen of them milling around as if waiting for a command to spring into action.

I watched one of them drift through the backyard toward the big maple. I thought for a moment that it was going to crash into the trunk, but it continued right on through it like a ghost passing through a wall.

Switching to another window I saw a large group of orbs on the front step. One of them slid through the front door as if it were a bead curtain. Then the others followed.

"In another minute this place will be swarming with time police! Are you coming or not?" I called to Zoe.

Zoe gave me a look that could instantly chill molten lava into cold, hard stone. "Sorry, you can go by yourself."

"But with *this* I can solve the time-warp factor." I held up the time machine. "I know I can!"

"I'm sure it's possible," said Zoe. "And maybe you can give these time cops the slip, too. But I'm not going anywhere with anyone who can lie as cruelly as you do!"

I couldn't believe what I was hearing. It just didn't seem reasonable for anyone to be hung up on one little lie — especially to the creep!

"You don't understand," I explained. "The little punk drives me crazy. Even when he's trying to be nice, he makes my skin crawl."

"You're the one who doesn't understand," said Zoe. "Can't you see how he looks up to you? How he trusts you?"

"A few minutes ago he nearly killed you. And now you're defending him? It doesn't make sense!"

"At least he said he was sorry," said Zoe. "That's more than you ever do!"

"Look, he'll get over it!" I was nearly begging now. "He's used to me lying to him. Really."

"Maybe he will," said Zoe as she crossed her arms over her chest. "But I won't!"

She had a steely glint in her eyes that said "Never!"

I knew I had to give in or go alone.

"So you'll come if we take Jonathan with us? You promise?" I asked.

Zoe didn't hesitate for a second. "Yes," she said. "That's the only way you'll get me inside that spaceship!"

I could feel the seconds ticking away. We had to leave right now.

For all I knew the time police had mind erasers. They might be able to perform some kind of lobotomy on my brain and take away my amazing intellect so I'd never bother them again.

Then it hit me — a way I could meet Zoe's demand and not have to deal with the creep. Honestly, sometimes I think my genius works best under pressure!

"Good," I said and ran to Star Jumper's cargo hold. In a compartment in a locked box I keep Star Jumper's main security device: the Micro-Blaster.

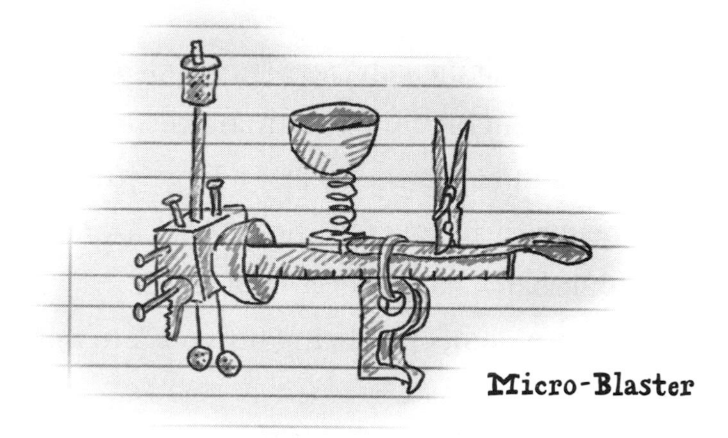

I quickly unlocked the box with the secret combination, took out the Blaster and turned it on.

"Follow me," I said and raced down the hall to Jonathan's room.

Jonathan was already inside his cardboard castle, no doubt "consulting with Merlin." I raised the Micro-Blaster and pointed it dead center at the castle door.

"What are you doing?" cried Zoe.

"Keeping my part of the bargain," I said and pulled the trigger. There was a whining sound as the Blaster built up a charge. Then *POOF*! A small pink flash went off, and Jonathan's castle was instantly reduced to the size of a large yo-yo.

Zoe nearly fell over in shock.

"Jonathan was in there!" she cried.

"No problem. I can bring him back to normal size whenever I want."

(The Micro-Blaster works on the principal of reducing the space between atoms. So it can shrink or expand anything without changing its essential nature. If I do say so myself, it's one of my neatest inventions!)

I grabbed the mayonnaise jar on Jonathan's windowsill. (Dad had helped him poke some holes in the lid of the jar so he could keep a pet cricket in it. Jonathan caught a cricket by himself but forgot to give it something to eat. When the poor bug starved to death, Jonathan refused to believe it was dead, insisting, "He's sleeping, that's all.")

While Zoe stood with her mouth wide open, I quickly unscrewed the lid, dumped the dead cricket out and picked up Jonathan's tiny castle. Then I gently slid it into the jar and screwed the lid back on.

"Okay," I said. "Now I have Jonathan. Let's go."

Zoe was still in a state of shock and bewilderment.

"But … but Jonathan was in his castle," she said again.

"I told you — I can make him normal sized again whenever I want."

"But why, Alex?" she gasped. "Why would you do such a thing?"

"Jonathan's fine," I insisted. "And this way he won't be such a pest."

I held up the jar, and we both watched as a one-inch-tall Jonathan crawled out of his castle. He waved his arms and shouted at us, but all I could make out were some squeaky noises.

"You see, he's fine," I said.

Just then a tiny figure squeezed out of the castle and stood beside Jonathan. It was a thin, bearded old man wearing a purple robe and a pointed hat.

Now *I* was the one who was shocked. I never dreamed that Jonathan's babble about talking to Merlin could be real. For a split second I thought I was hallucinating.

"Who's *he?*" gasped Zoe. "Merlin?"

"Never mind about that!" I cried. "For the final time — are you coming or not?"

Zoe didn't answer with words. But by the way she sighed and the look she gave me I knew her answer was yes.

By then all the time cops had entered the house. I saw the first one just as we left Jonathan's room. It had floated up the stairs and was turning down the hall.

"STOP!" it announced in a loud, authoritarian voice. "YOU ARE BEING DETAINED FOR VIOLATION OF RULE 31 OF THE UNIFORM TIME-CODE."

"Sorry, officer," I said as we slowly backed down the hall into my room. "Just let me get some of my things."

"STOP!" cried the time cop in the exact same voice as before. "I REPEAT: YOU ARE BEING DETAINED FOR VIOLATION OF RULE 31 OF THE UNIFORM TIME-CODE."

As we inched into my room, three more time cops drifted through the walls. All of them were saying the same thing as the first cop in the exact same voice.

"Move very slowly," I said under my breath to Zoe as I passed her the mayonnaise jar. "No sudden moves. Just get in Star Jumper. Turn on all systems and rev up the Float-Mode gyros."

As Zoe backed slowly into the spaceship, I held up the time machine. "This is what you want, isn't it?" I said.

Several more time police floated through the walls. My room was starting to get really crowded.

"AFFIRMATIVE!" they all said in unison.

"No problem," I replied. "Just one second while I get something."

I held up my Micro-Blaster and adjusted its focus and range. I wasn't going to do anything unless they tried to stop me.

Then I saw a bright red glow shining through their black plastic surfaces. It looked as if they were revving up some kind of stun ray.

"STOP OR WE WILL BE FORCED TO IMMOBILIZE YOU," said one of the robots.

I calibrated the Blaster to shrink the robots to a size invisible to the naked eye, pulled the trigger and swept it around the room.

Zaaaaap! There was the usual pink flash, but nothing happened.

"Rotten wormholes!" I cursed under my breath. "They must have a built-in shield!"

Once again I was drawn to the orbs' peculiar antenna arrangement. "I know I've seen that before," I said to myself. It seemed like a really stupid time to be distracted by something like that. But I couldn't help it. Then it hit me. *For crying out loud,* I thought. I *designed those antennas.* I *designed those orbs!*

What I was up against became clear to me in an instant. The time police were based on the spherical robots I had planned to build someday. Once again, someone in the future had used my designs!

I dropped my Blaster.

"I won't resist any further," I said. "I just want to show you something."

One of the robots suddenly emitted a tractor beam that raised the Micro-Blaster off the floor.

"WE WILL ALLOW YOU TO SHOW US SOMETHING AS LONG AS THAT ACTION DOES NOT BECOME THREATENING TO OUR MISSION," said the robotic sphere in an emotionless monotone.

I walked over to my desk and opened my "New Concepts" notebook.

"You see?" I held it up. "It's just a book."

I opened the notebook to the pages where I had created the designs and written down the essential formulas for the orbs.

"Your existence is based on the existence of these drawings," I said as I ripped the pages from the notebook and then tore them in half and half again. "And now that they no longer exist and I resolve never to design them again, all of you will also cease to exist!"

It was a long shot, but it worked. The time police slowly faded and then popped like bubbles.

"Amazing!" I gasped. I had successfully used a time paradox to my own benefit. But I had no idea how long the effect would last. Any minute now, time police of some other design could take the place of the ones I had assigned to oblivion.

There wasn't a moment to lose. I snatched up the Micro-Blaster and shoved it in my belt. Then I dove into Star Jumper and locked the hatch behind me.

"Get us out of here!" I cried.

"Aye, aye, Captain!" answered Zoe. And a nanosecond later we slipped into hyper-space and star-jumped trillions of miles away from Earth!

EPILOGUE

Time Will Tell

A good planet is hard to find.

So far we've looked at eight. Three of them had atmospheres that were unbreathable. X-4 revolved so slowly its daytime surface temperature topped 300 degrees, and every night its tiny pools of water froze solid. X-5 was constantly swept with violent hurricanes. X-6 had lots of good water and a nice climate but no life-forms more complicated than single-celled amoebas. X-7 was undergoing violent volcanic eruptions. And X-8 had been contaminated with lethal levels of radiation, apparently the result of a devastating nuclear war.

As I write these words, Zoe is taking a nap in the sleep port beneath me. I can hear her slow, even breathing through Star Jumper's thin cardboard walls. There's also the hum of the auxiliary computer as it runs atmosphere and life-form scans on X-9. (Hmm … I just noticed a subtle wheeze in the air-circulation system. I have to look into that soon, before a real problem develops.)

Out of Star Jumper's main portal I can see X-9's iridescent blue and white surface turning slowly beneath us. Its continents are shaped differently, but it reminds me so much of Earth that I have to admit I feel a little homesick already — and we've only been gone nine days, seven hours and thirty-five minutes.

Planet X-9

X-9 has vast oceans and green continents like Earth. It has two polar ice caps and moderate weather patterns. I'm almost a hundred percent sure it supports life. But what sort of life? Advanced or primitive? When Zoe wakes up and we go down to the surface will amoebas, dinosaurs or highly developed humanoids be there to greet us?

I've been waiting and working for this moment for so long I'm tempted to wake Zoe up right now. But the ship's computer is still running some important tests.

Jonathan? He's still in the mayonnaise jar, angry as a stirred-up bumblebee. I would have brought him back to normal size earlier, but Star Jumper wasn't designed to transport three. If I made him normal size again he'd have to sleep in the cargo hold. And that's already crowded with gear and stuff. And he loves his castle. There's no way I could make that actual size again — not in the ship, at least. Also, because we had to leave on such short notice we're not completely outfitted with full food rations. So keeping Jonathan small makes our space grub last longer.

All of those are good reasons. But the real reason is a lot simpler. This way he's out of my hair. Of course, I did promise Zoe I'd bring him back to normal when we found a planet worth exploring.

If you're wondering about Merlin, well, so am I.

Every once in a while I see him and Jonathan having picnics out in front of the castle. I guess Merlin brings the food.

Sometimes I'm tempted to make myself small with the Micro-Blaster and go inside the jar and talk to Merlin. But so far I've been too busy running the ship and sorting out planets.

As for the time machine, I've already made a duplicate with the extra stuff I brought along. It's a little bit bigger than the device we got from the lady in the park. But it works just fine. After we get settled into a new planet I'll go back to the time just before she woke up and return her machine.

So far the time police haven't tracked us. But if they do, you can bet your last photon that I'm more than ready for them.

Ah! The life scanners have just finished their calculations. And the results are (at a glance) excellent! According to the data, X-9 is teeming with all kinds of highly advanced life-forms!

Time to wake up Zoe and go exploring! And maybe, just maybe, time to let Jonathan out of his jar …